Sunshine was a girl wh[o was] full of energy and excite[ment.] truly made Sunshine s[parkle was her] love for one thing above all else – helping others!

One evening, Sunshine was in the kitchen with her mom as usual. She bounced on her toes, her eyes wide with anticipation. "Mommy, what can I do to help again?" she asked, her voice bubbling with excitement.

Mom chuckled at her daughter's enthusiasm. "Oh, Sunshine, thank you for helping me clear the table and assisting with dinner tonight! But now, it's time for you to go to bed, school awaits tomorrow."

Sunshine's face fell for a moment, but then she brightened up again. "But Mommy, can I wash the dishes then? Pleeease?"

Mom couldn't resist Sunshine's puppy eyes. "Alright, Sunshine. How about you help me with the red beans for tomorrow's dinner, and that's it?"

"Red beans and rice? Yay!" Sunshine exclaimed, clapping her hands together in delight. "Thank you, Mommy! You're the best!"

With a skip in her step, Sunshine hurried to the pantry, her heart racing with excitement. She needed no help finding these things because her mom made red beans and rice every Monday - a tradition in her house and almost every home in New Orleans and beyond.

First, she reached for her favorite bowl, the one her mom always used for cleaning beans. The bowl was smooth and slightly chipped on one edge, a testament to its frequent use.

"Red beans, oh red beans, where are you hiding?" she sang, her voice echoing through the kitchen as she searched through the pantry. She pushed aside bags of rice and jars of spices until she found the familiar bag of red beans hiding among the other ingredients.

"Gotcha!" Sunshine cheered, triumphantly holding up the bag of red beans in the air. "It's time to get soaked!"

And with that, Sunshine set to work, cleaning the beans with all the care and attention. As she worked, she hummed a happy tune, as she imagined herself eating delicious dinner that awaited them the next day.

"Look, Mommy! No rocks!" Sunshine exclaimed proudly, holding up the beans for her mom to see. "The beans are all clean and soaking for tomorrow!"

Her mom smiled, ruffling Sunshine's hair affectionately. "Well done, Sunshine! You're a natural in the kitchen."

Sunshine grinned from ear to ear, her heart swelling with pride. Soon, it was time for Sunshine to say goodbye to her beloved kitchen and go to bed.

"Aw, Mommy, do I really have to go to bed already?" Sunshine pouted, her bottom lip sticking out in a playful pout.

Her mom chuckled softly, wrapping her arms around Sunshine in a warm embrace. "I'm afraid so, my little sunshine. It's time for bed," she said, her voice soft and soothing.

"Goodnight, kitchen. I'll see you in the morning," she whispered with a sigh, pressing a tender kiss to the countertop before turning to follow her mom up the stairs.

Once in her bedroom, Sunshine snuggled under the covers, her eyes shining with anticipation. "Mommy, will you read me a story tonight?" she asked, her voice filled with excitement.

Her mom smiled. "Of course, sweetheart. Which story would you like to hear?"

Before answering Sunshine's voice softened, "First I want to say, thank you again, Mom, for letting me help in the kitchen. It makes me so happy. I love you mom.

"You're welcome my Beautiful Sunshine, I love you too!"

Now, can you read the new book we got from the library, 'The Perfect Picnic'?" she asked, bouncing up and down with excitement.

Her mom laughed, flipping open the book to the first page. "Absolutely! Now snuggle up tight and get ready for an adventure!"

And so, with Sunshine cuddling in her arms, her mom began to read, her voice as sweet as a song in Sunshine's ears.

As the story was coming to an end, Sunshine started to yawn, her eyelids growing heavy.

...By the time the family made it home from the perfect picnic, everyone was worn out and ready for bed, just like I hope that you're ready for bed, Sunshine." Mom looked down and saw that Sunshine was fast asleep!

Mom smiled, pressing a gentle kiss to Sunshine's forehead. "Sleep well, sweetheart. Tomorrow is a brand new day, filled with many possibilities.

The next morning, Sunshine was still in bed when she heard her mom's voice.

"Sunshine, wake up! Time for school!" Mom called.

"Good morning, Mommy. Is this why people say they don't like Mondays?" Sunshine asked as she stretched her body

Mom laughed, "Mondays need a little extra push sometimes. But after you wake up, brush your teeth, smile, and give thanks, you'll be ready for a great day."

"Okay, mommy!" Sunshine answered with a nod.

"Now, breakfast is ready! I made your favorite," Mom announced.

"Eggs and rice, Mom? Yum! You always know how to make my mornings happy!" Sunshine exclaimed, digging into her breakfast with joy.

Sunshine's day was off to a good start; she was all smiles as she drove to school with her mom, ready to conquer another exciting day.

As they pulled up to the school, Sunshine's mom reminded her of their morning mantra: "Have a great day, and be the joy, light, and love that you are!"

"I will, Mommy! And I'll leave a little with you!" Sunshine said as she exited the car, stopping in her tracks. "Oh, Mom?"

"Yes, Sunshine?" her mom answered.

"Can I ride the school bus home today?" Sunshine pleaded.

"Yes, you can," said Mom.

"Yay! Thank you, Mommy!" Sunshine squealed.

Skipping into the schoolyard, she spread her infectious energy. "Hey y'all! Happy Monday! I missed y'all so much!" She greeted her friends with hugs and high-fives, drawing smiles from her teachers.

Yet, as Sunshine looked around, she spotted her friend Allen, who seemed quieter than usual. His head hung low, and Sunshine sensed something was bothering him.

"Allen, are you OK?" she asked, concerned.
"I'm not having a good day, Sunshine," he replied,
with his head down.


The school bell rang, ending the morning chatter,
and their teacher, Miss No'La, directed them
to their class.

"Good morning, everyone! Please take a seat and take out your supplies," said Miss No'La. "Today, we will talk about what we did over the weekend."

Eager students shared their adventures, but when it was De'Lis's turn, she admitted, "My weekend wasn't great. My friend's slumber party got canceled, and I didn't do anything fun."

Sunshine, always ready to spread joy, whispered to De'Lis on her way back to her seat, "My mom is cooking red beans and rice for dinner—it's always fun. You can come! This can make up for the weekend."

De'Lis smiled, cheered by Sunshine's kindness. "Thank you, Sunshine. I'd love to."

When it was Sunshine's turn, she shared her weekend stories, from parades to the zoo and library, with crawfish and beignets adding a delicious twist. The grand finale? Helping with dinner and getting the beans ready for tonight.

"It was so much fun!!" Sunshine said, sparking cheers from the whole class.

But the day held more surprises. The intercom buzzed, and Ms. Green, the school principal, shared exciting news.

"Excuse me, Miss No'La, your class has been selected for Good Deed Monday. Can you send two students to help the 6th graders pass out this week's newsletter?"

"Me! Me! Me!" echoed through the class as everyone raised their hands.

"Sunshine, Allen, can you clear your desk and head to the office to help with Good Deed Monday, please?" Miss No'La said.

Sunshine and Allen did as their teacher had commanded. While Sunshine was excited, Allen was still droopy.

Sunshine turned to Allen with a bright smile as they made their way down the hall. "Come on, Allen! Let's go! They're waiting!"

"Okayyyy," Allen replied, his spirits low as he shuffled along behind her.

"Allen, Miss No'La trusted us for Good Deed Monday. Aren't you happy?" Sunshine asked, her voice filled with warmth and encouragement.

"Sunshine, I don't know if I should be happy or not. My best friend who lives next door is moving, and I'm going to miss him," Allen sighed.

"Allen, I'll be your best friend. Guess what? My mom is cooking red beans and rice for dinner; you can come tonight. It might make you feel better. It always makes me feel better," Sunshine offered, hoping to lift his spirits.

"Sunshine, my mom is cooking red beans and rice too!" Allen replied, seeming irritated.

"But it's always fun at my house, Allen. My mom plays music, I dance, and she lets me help in the kitchen," Sunshine added.

As they entered the office, a curious student asked Allen, "Why the pout?" Before he could respond, Sunshine jumped in, speaking up for him.

After hearing about his disappointment, the students offered encouragement, assuring Allen that things would get better. They let him know that as you get older, you meet new friends and often reconnect with old friends.

"Now, let's get started. This will take us until lunchtime," Sunshine declared, eager to lend a hand.

Amidst the chatter, one of the older students mentioned they were hungry because they did not have time to eat breakfast due to last-minute homework assignment.

"My mom can help you with your homework, she is good at that," Sunshine suggested. "You can come tonight; and she's cooking red beans and rice for dinner."

"Aww, how sweet. I see why your name is Sunshine," one of the older students said, touched by her kindness.

As their task came to an end, they beamed at Sunshine and Allen, "Wasn't that fun?

We're glad you came around.

Thank you both for your help. Do you need us to walk you back to class?"

"No, we're okay," Sunshine replied politely.

As Sunshine and Allen stepped back into the classroom, they were greeted by Miss No'La's announcement, "Just in time for lunch and recess; how was it?


Wait, you can share when we come back from lunch."

On the way to lunch, Sunshine stopped in her tracks and her heart leaped with joy as she spotted her favorite person in the school, Ms. Mae, the school's custodian. "Is that my favorite Sunshine? I missed you!"

"Ms. Mae, I missed you! Guess what? My mom is cooking red beans and rice for dinner; you can come," Sunshine announced with a wink.

"Aww, how sweet of you, Sunshine! Enjoy your lunch and don't lose that sunshine," Ms. Mae replied, her eyes twinkling with affection.

As Sunshine and her classmates made their way to the bus line, she couldn't contain her joy. "Wow! This is the best Monday ever!"

"Happy Monday!" Sunshine called out to Mr. Saint, the bus driver, as she hopped onto the bus.

"Looks like someone had a good day! Hi, Sunshine!" Mr. Saint greeted her warmly.

"My mom is cooking red beans and rice for dinner, you can come," Sunshine offered with a grin.

"You are a sweet girl, Sunshine!" Mr. Saint replied with a chuckle.

As Sunshine burst through the door at home, her excitement bubbling over, she called out, "Mommy, I'm home!"

"I'm in the kitchen," her mom replied, her voice filled with warmth.

"How was your day?" Sunshine's mom asked as she stood at the stove frying chicken.

"Today was the best day ever!" Sunshine exclaimed. "I was chosen for Good Deed Monday!"

"Wow, baby! Congratulations!" Mom said proudly.

"Well, do you want to wash up and help set the table?" her mom asked with a smile. "I'm frying the last few pieces of chicken so we can sit down at the table and hear about the rest of your exciting day."

"Yes, I do, Mommy," Sunshine replied eagerly.

As Sunshine was placing the final dish on the table, the doorbell rang. Sunshine's mom wondered aloud,


"Who could that be? I'm not expecting anyone." The doorbell rang once again, adding to the mystery.

Opening the door, she was greeted by Allen. "Hi, Ms. Joy. Sunshine invited me over for red beans and rice," he explained shyly.

"Oh!" Sunshine's mom exclaimed, surprised and delighted that Sunshine had thought of her friend. "Come in, wash your hands, and have a seat. I'm just now serving the food."

"Allen! I'm so happy you made it!" Sunshine exclaimed with joy. "I set the table; you like it?"

"I do, Sunshine," Allen replied with a smile, taking in the inviting setup. "And the food smells so good."

"Allen, do you want any...?" Sunshine's mom began, but before she could finish, the doorbell rang again.

Curious, Sunshine's mom opened the door to find Miss No'La and Ms. Mae standing there. "Is everything okay?" she asked, surprised by their unexpected visit.

"Yes, Sunshine didn't tell you she invited us to dinner?" Ms. Mae chimed in.

"Sunshine is full of surprises today, but there's plenty, and you are always welcome," Sunshine's mom said with a laugh. "Come, everyone is in the kitchen."

But the surprises didn't end there. Just as Sunshine's mom was getting over the shock of unexpected guests, there came another knock at the door.

"Who else could it be? Sunshine, did you invite the whole school?" she teased, chuckling as she headed to the door.

"Heyyyy!! Look who I found," Mr. Saint announced, pointing to De'Lis and one of the students who Sunshine had helped during Good Deed Monday.

"Hi, Sunshine invited us over for red beans and rice," they explained.

"Come right on in; we're just getting started," Sunshine's mom welcomed them warmly. "Mommy, this is everyone that I invited to dinner." Sunshine stated.

As the guests settled in at the table, Sunshine's heart swelled with happiness. She had wanted to make this dinner special for everyone, and now, with guests filling their home, she knew she had succeeded.

But as the evening went on, Sunshine couldn't help but worry that her mom might be overwhelmed by the unexpected company.

"Mommy, are you okay?" she whispered, her voice filled with concern.

Sunshine's mom smiled, her eyes twinkling with pride. "I'm more than okay, Sunshine," she replied, her voice filled with love. "I'm so proud of you for inviting your friends to dinner. You've made this evening truly special."

With tears of joy in her eyes, Sunshine hugged her mom tight, her heart overflowing with happiness. Tonight may have started as a surprise, but it had turned into a night filled with love, laughter, and the warmth of community.

Laughter filled the air as they shared stories, jokes, and delicious food, their hearts overflowing with love and happiness.

"Pass the red beans, please!" Allen exclaimed, reaching across the table with a smile.

"Here you go!" Sunshine replied, her face beaming with joy as she handed him the bowl.

Sunshine's mom looked around the table, her heart swelling with pride. "Thank you all for joining us tonight," she said, her voice filled with gratitude. "This dinner is truly a celebration of love, kindness, and community."

Miss No'La nodded in agreement, her eyes shining with warmth. "Indeed it is, Ms. Joy. And we have Sunshine to thank for bringing us all together."

Sunshine blushed at the praise, her cheeks turning rosy with embarrassment. "Aw, shucks," she murmured, her heart filled with happiness.

As they continued to enjoy their meal, plates were passed, stories were shared, and bonds were strengthened, all thanks to Sunshine's simple act of kindness.

"Dinner was amazing, thank you for having us," said Ms. Mae.

"Yes, thank you, it was delicious," added De'Lis.

As the guests said their goodbyes, their bellies were full and their hearts even fuller, filled with love and gratitude for the precious moments they had shared.

Sunshine and her mom sat on the couch for a while, reflecting on the night. Sunshine's mom smiled, her eyes twinkling with happiness. "Tonight was truly special," she said, her voice filled with love. "And it's all thanks to our little Sunshine."

Sunshine beamed with pride, her heart beating with happiness. "I love you, Mommy," she whispered, wrapping her arms around her mom in a tight hug.

As they settled in for the night, their hearts full of love, Sunshine knew that no matter what tomorrow brought, as long as they had each other, they could weather any storm with love, kindness, and the warmth of community.

And so, with hearts full of gratitude and dreams full of possibilities, Sunshine drifted off to sleep, ready to face whatever adventures awaited her in the days to come.

Made in the USA
Columbia, SC
06 December 2024